JOEY

JACK KENT

Scholastic Inc.
New York   Toronto   London   Aukland   Sydney

ISBN 0-590-33678-9

Copyright © 1984 by Jack Kent.
All rights reserved. Published by Scholastic Inc.,
730 Broadway, New York, NY 10003, by arrangement
with Prentice-Hall, Inc.

12 11 10 9 8 7 6 5 4 3   9/8 0/9

Printed in the U.S.A.   08

To Naomi and Michael

Once there was a little kangaroo named Joey.
His mother worried about him, as mothers do.
She worried that Joey might get lost.

So, to keep track of him,
she put Joey in her pocket.

It was comfortable in mother's pocket. Joey had his coloring books and his toys to play with there. But he was lonely for someone his own age.

"I want to go play with my friends," said Joey.
"Ask your friends to come HERE and play," said mother.

So Joey invited his friend Billy.

And he invited his friend Betty.

And he invited his friend Bob.
And they all came to visit.

At first Joey's friends had fun bouncing around in mother's pocket.

But after a while they wanted to do
something else.
"Let's watch TV," said Billy.

"I don't have a TV," said Joey.
"I'll get mine," Billy said.

And he did.

At first they couldn't
get a good picture.

"Is that better?" asked Billy.
"Much better," said Bob.
"But there aren't any programs
worth watching," said Betty.

"Let's play some records."
"I don't have a record player,"
said Joey.
"I'll get my stereo," said Bob.

And he did.
Betty and Billy helped.

They listened to the music and danced.

"We've played all the records,"
said Billy. "Now what?"

"Let's form a band and play our OWN music," said Betty. "I have a guitar," said Joey.

Billy and Betty and Bob
ran to get their instruments.

Bob brought his horn.

Billy brought his drums.

And Betty brought her piano.

"THAT WILL DO!"

said mother.

"OUT! OUT! Everybody out!" she said
Out went the TV and the stereo. Out went Bob and his horn.

Out went Billy and his drums.

Out went Betty and her piano.